THE PALADIN'S HANDBOOK

OFFICIAL GUIDEBOOK OF *VOLTRON LEGENDARY DEFENDER*

SIMON SPOTLIGHT
An imprint of Simon & Schuster Children's Publishing Division
1230 Avenue of the Americas, New York, New York 10020
This Simon Spotlight paperback edition August 2017
DreamWorks Voltron Legendary Defender © 2017 DreamWorks Animation LLC. TM
World Events Productions, LLC. All Rights Reserved. All rights reserved, including
the right of reproduction in whole or in part in any form. SIMON SPOTLIGHT and
colophon are registered trademarks of Simon & Schuster, Inc. For information
about special discounts for bulk purchases, please contact Simon & Schuster
Special Sales at 1-866-506-1949 or business@simonandschuster.com.
Designed by Julie Robine
Manufactured in the United States of America 0717 LAK
10 9 8 7 6 5 4 3 2 1
ISBN 978-1-5344-0903-3
ISBN 978-1-5344-0904-0 (eBook)

CONTENTS

Welcome, Young Paladin!

Greetings. I am Princess Allura of Planet Altea. Ten thousand years ago, my father created Voltron, the most powerful weapon in the universe. It takes five brave Paladins to pilot the lions that come together to form Voltron. The Paladins of Voltron have an important task: Defend the universe, no matter the cost. In this handbook, you will find everything you need to know about being a Paladin of Voltron. I have ~~asked~~ FORCED our current Paladins to help assemble this guidebook. It is our hope these notes assist you on your Paladin journey. Please remember: you must treat this guidebook CAREFULLY. Do NOT leave it out in the open, lest you risk it falling into enemy hands.

The fate of the universe lies with Voltron—and with you.

HUNK Lance Keith
Pidge Shiro
Allura Coran

MEET THE LIONS

When the lions combine, they form Voltron—the Defender of the Universe. Each lion possesses its own unique personality and abilities. Here you will find a breakdown of the lions.

ASSUMING KEITH DOESN'T RUN OFF OR SOMETHING. OR GETS STUCK ON A TACO PLANET.

BLACK LION

Guardian Spirit of the Cosmos

Voltron Position: head and torso
Found: Castle of Lions

The Black Lion is the head and torso of Voltron. It chooses a pilot who is a born leader—calm and in control at all times. Someone whose team will follow without hesitation.

The Black Lion is the largest, smartest, and most powerful of all the lions. It is also the most difficult to fly.

DAMAGE //////////////////////00000

ARMOR //////////////////////00000

SPEED ///////////////////////00000

CAPABILITIES

- **Tail Laser:** moderately damages targets at long range
- **Mouth Cannon:** severely damages targets at long range
- **Jaw Blade:** cuts through targets at very close range
- **Hidden Power:** Ephemeral Blades. These wings can vanquish an enemy instantly and permit the Black Lion to pass through solid objects.

RED LION

Guardian Spirit of the Core

Voltron Position: right arm
Found: Galra battleship

DAMAGE ///////////0000000000

ARMOR //////////////0000000

SPEED /////////////////////

The Red Lion is temperamental. It is faster and more agile than the others but also more unstable. It chooses a pilot who relies more on instincts than skills alone.

The Red Lion can withstand extremely high temperatures and is capable of supersonic speeds. If flying close to a supernova, the Red Lion gets the call.

CAPABILITIES

- **Tail Laser:** moderately damages targets at long range
- **Mouth Cannon:** severely damages targets at long range
- **Jaw Blade:** cuts through targets at very close range
- **Magma Beam:** disintegrates target on contact
  - **Hidden Power:** The Red Lion activates a plasma cannon.

GREEN LION

Guardian Spirit of the Forest

Voltron Position: left arm
Found: remote jungle planet

The Green Lion has a curious personality. It chooses a pilot of intellect and daring. As an arm of Voltron, the Green Lion is one of the smallest lions. However, it is a fierce opponent and a protective ally. With its stealth capabilities, the Green Lion can appear without warning and befuddle the most devious of foes.

DAMAGE //////////////

ARMOR //////////////////

SPEED ////////////////////

CAPABILITIES

- **Tail Laser:** moderately damages targets at long range
- **Mouth Cannon:** severely damages targets at long range
- **Jaw Blade:** cuts through targets at very close range
- **Short-term cloaking shield**
- **Hidden Power:** Vine Cannon, which creates enormous, strong vines to trap enemies or support structures

Well, this one I added.

ONCE, IT SEWED TOGETHER THE SURFACE OF A WHOLE PLANET!

BLUE LION

Guardian Spirit of the Water

Voltron Position: right leg
Found: Earth

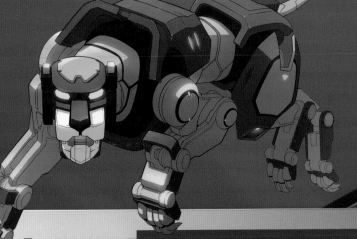

The Blue Lion has a friendly nature. It has an adventurous spirit and chooses a pilot who is equally bold.

DAMAGE //////////////////000000

ARMOR //////////////////000000

SPEED //////////////////00000

The Blue Lion is one of the larger Voltron ships. It is at home in the water and can withstand intense atmospheric pressure. It is also the most accepting of new pilots.

BLUE! I THOUGHT WHAT WE HAD WAS SPECIAL.

CAPABILITIES

- **Tail Laser:** moderately damages targets at long range
- **Mouth Cannon:** severely damages targets at long range
- **Jaw Blade:** cuts through targets at very close range
- **Ice Ray:** freezes long-range targets on contact
  - **Hidden Power:** Sonic Cannon, used to repel enemies and echolocate

YELLOW LION

Guardian Spirit of the Land

Voltron Position: left leg
Found: below a Galra mining planet

DAMAGE ///////////////////
ARMOR ///////////////////////
SPEED ////////////////

The Yellow Lion is caring and kind. It chooses a pilot who puts the needs of others first and carries a mighty heart. As a leg of Voltron, the Yellow Lion is one of the larger ships. It is dependable, tough, and strong. It can take more firepower than the other lions and packs enough force to break through solid rock.

CAPABILITIES

- **Tail Laser:** moderately damages targets a long range
- **Mouth Cannon:** severely damages targets at long range
- **Jaw Blade:** cuts through targets at very close range
- **Hidden Power:** under extreme pressure, the Yellow Lion activates hidden side thrusters and longer, stronger armor claws. Hunk's upgrade also allows him access to bulked-up armor plating.

MEET THE PALADINS

Really, Hunk? I give you my camera and THIS is the photo you choose?

I LOOK SO STUDIOUS
IT'S A GREAT PHOTO
REALLY CAPTURES W
WE ARE, YOU KNO

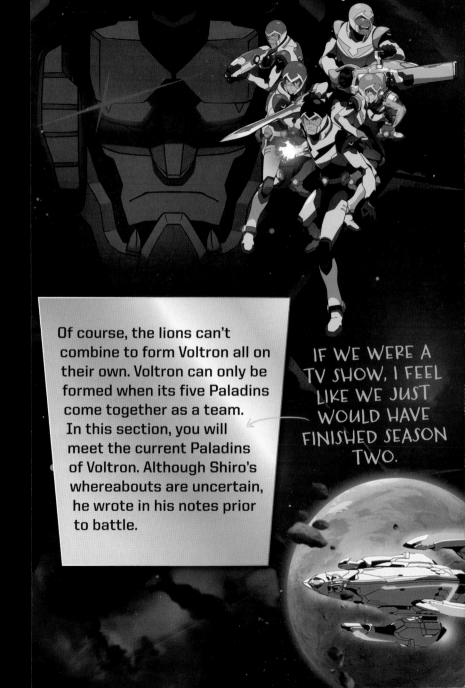

Of course, the lions can't combine to form Voltron all on their own. Voltron can only be formed when its five Paladins come together as a team. In this section, you will meet the current Paladins of Voltron. Although Shiro's whereabouts are uncertain, he wrote in his notes prior to battle.

IF WE WERE A TV SHOW, I FEEL LIKE WE JUST WOULD HAVE FINISHED SEASON TWO.

SHIRO

"SPACE DAD"

The oldest and most
experienced pilot of the
current Paladins of Voltron,
Shiro is bonded to the Black Lion.

STATS

- Full name: Takashi Shirogane
- Birthday: February 29
- Heritage: Japanese
- Age: 25

STRENGTH ////////////////////////

AGILITY ////////////////////////

INTELLIGENCE ////////////////////////

BACKSTORY

Before becoming a Voltron Paladin, Shiro was a
skilled exploration pilot. Shiro was collecting ice
samples on the Kerberos Mission when he was
captured by the Galra Empire. See "Kerberos Mission
 The Galra trained Shiro   File" on page 82 for more
to be a gladiator and outfitted him with information.
a robotic arm. About a year later, Shiro escaped
the Galra and returned to Earth in an escape
pod. He crash-landed right outside of the
Galaxy Garrison, where he was found by the
other soon-to-be Paladins.

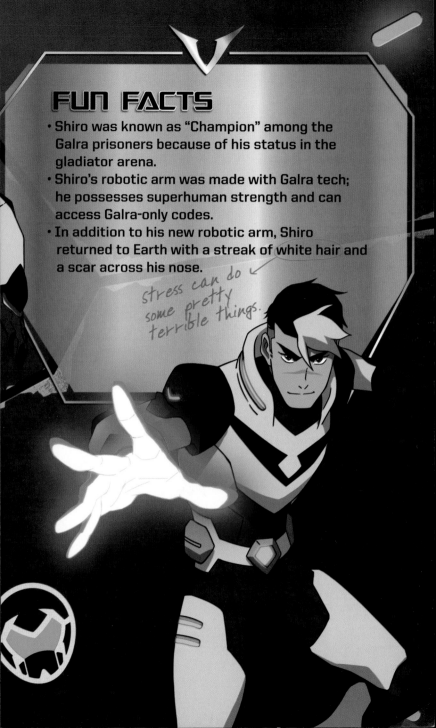

FUN FACTS

- Shiro was known as "Champion" among the Galra prisoners because of his status in the gladiator arena.
- Shiro's robotic arm was made with Galra tech; he possesses superhuman strength and can access Galra-only codes.
- In addition to his new robotic arm, Shiro returned to Earth with a streak of white hair and a scar across his nose.

stress can do some pretty terrible things.

KEITH

Ugh. This guy.

Keith was the most talented fighter pilot at the Galaxy Garrison, but flunked out due to a discipline issue. Keith is bonded to the Red Lion.

STATS

- Member of the Blade of Marmora
- Birthday: October 23
- Heritage: part human, part Galra
- Age: 18

Hair: really bad mullet. No bueno for the ladies. Enough with my hair already!

STRENGTH	///////////////////oooooooo
AGILITY	//////////////////////////
INTELLIGENCE	///////////////////oooooo

BACKSTORY

After getting booted fom the Galaxy Garrison, Keith lived in a desert shack where he discovered the cave where the Blue Lion was hidden. Keith is part Galra, but his family history remains a mystery.

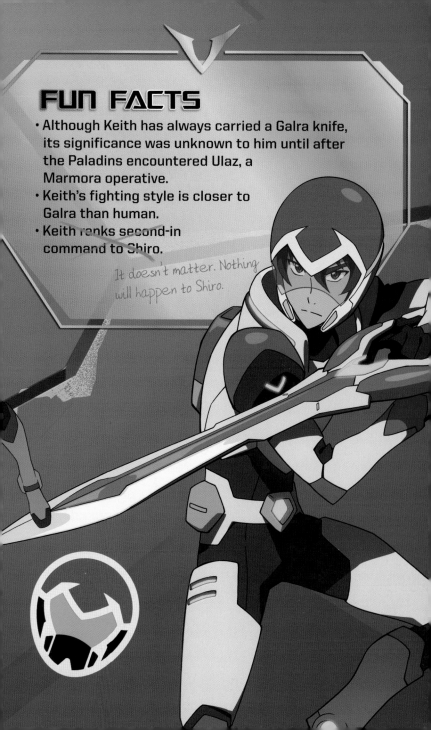

FUN FACTS

- Although Keith has always carried a Galra knife, its significance was unknown to him until after the Paladins encountered Ulaz, a Marmora operative.
- Keith's fighting style is closer to Galra than human.
- Keith ranks second-in command to Shiro.

It doesn't matter. Nothing will happen to Shiro.

PIDGE

A technological genius and the youngest Paladin on the team, Pidge is known for her smarts and quick wit. Pidge is bonded to the Green Lion.

STATS

- Full name: Katie Holt
- Birthday: April 3
- Heritage: Italian
- Age: 15

WAIT, IT'S NOT PIDGE GUNDERSON?

Pidge is my alias, Hunk!

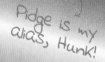

FUN FACTS

- Pidge once reprogrammed a Galra drone to be her assistant and named it Rover.
- Pidge really loves peanut butter cookies—but not peanuts!
- Pidge is the shortest of the Paladins, which earns her the nickname "Number Five" from Coran.

BACKSTORY

When Pidge was fourteen, her father and brother left for space on the Kerberos Mission. Soon after, though, the crewmembers stopped sending signals. Everyone believed they were dead—everyone except Pidge.

Pidge, then known as Katie, hacked into confidential information stored on a Galaxy Garrison computer. However, she was caught and banned from the Garrison forever. Eager to find her family and discover the truth about what happened to them, Katie cut her hair and enrolled in the Garrison as a computer specialist, under the male alias "Pidge."

STRENGTH ///////// ◌◌◌◌◌◌◌◌◌◌◌◌

AGILITY ////////////////// ◌◌◌◌◌◌

INTELLIGENCE ////////////////////////

LANCE

THE MOST HANDSOME AND
SKILLFUL OF THE BUNCH.

A class clown and the most
eager to prove himself,
Lance is bonded to the
Blue Lion.

STATS

- Favorite food: garlic knots
- Birthday: July 28
- Heritage: Cuban
- Age: 17

STRENGTH //////////////////////
AGILITY //////////////////////
INTELLIGENCE ////////////////////////

BACKSTORY

Lance, Hunk, and Pidge were partaking
in an unauthorized "team-bonding
exercise" when they accidentally
watched Shiro's escape pod crash
to Earth. It was then that the future
Paladins came together for the first
time.

Once the team discovered the Blue
Lion, Lance instantly bonded with it.
Lance was the first Paladin to feel his
lion telepathically communicate—and
fly it!

FUN FACTS

- Like Pidge, Lance *loves* retro Earth video games.
- Lance's desire to make friends once got him captured by merpeople. But then we freed them and made a new alliance! Oh yeah. Who did that? Lancey Lance did that.
- Lance owns a pair of fuzzy Blue Lion slippers.

Actually, we all do. Lance just wears his the most.

HUNK

A compassionate pilot with a laid-back personality, Hunk is also a master chef. He is bonded to the Yellow Lion.

STATS

- Catchphrase: "I'm a leg!"
- Birthday: January 13
- Heritage: Samoan
- Age: 17

FUN FACTS

- Hunk has an encyclopedic knowledge of Earth spices and a growing understanding of herbs from other planets.
- Hunk has a knack for stating the obvious, such as "We're in some kind of futuristic alien cat head right now."
- If Hunk were stranded on a scary gas planet and had only one food to eat for the rest of his life, his choice would be a burrito.

STRENGTH /////////////////////
AGILITY ///////////////////
INTELLIGENCE /////////////////////

BACKSTORY

Hunk was a cadet in good academic standing at the Galaxy Garrison, but he often failed simulator flights due to motion sickness. *He threw up a lot.*

His skills were better applied on solid ground, where he could study flight without experiencing it.

When the team first came together, it was Hunk who identified the Fraunhofer line that brought them to the Blue Lion. Though he really was only looking for a candy bar!

BAYARDS

The Bayards are the traditional weapons of the Paladins of Voltron. They serve two functions: form unique, powerful weapons for each of the Paladins and provide upgrades to Voltron when inserted into their respective Bayard Ports.

GREEN BAYARD

- has hand blades and forms an electrified-edged grapple line
- for hand-to-hand combat

BLUE BAYARD

- an energy blaster
- precision targeting

RED BAYARD

- forms a sword
- close-range combat

YELLOW BAYARD

- forms a blaster
- energy cannon for long-range blasts

BLACK BAYARD

- forms an energy shield, sword, cannon, chain sword, large mace, and large sword

VOLTRON

Voltron is a fearsome robot created when the five lions (and Paladins) come together in an impressive feat of teamwork. Voltron is strong and resilient, and Voltron is the universe's last resort.

DAMAGE ///////////////////////////

ARMOR ///////////////////////////

SPEED ///////////////////////////

CAPABILITIES

SWORD: formed from the Red Paladin's Bayard, the sword is strong enough to cut through the exterior of an enemy ship. When combined with the Blue and Black Bayards, the sword grows in size and strength. The Green Bayard forms the sword. Surrounded by an energy aura, it is able to slice through a Galra battleship with one blow. When the Black Paladin's Bayard is engaged, Voltron forms a blazing sword, the most powerful weapon of all.

SHIELD: formed from the Black Lion's wings, the shield protects Voltron from enemy laser blasts.

LASERS: generated by both the Red and Green Lions, the lasers are effective long-range weapons.

SHOULDER CANNON: formed from the Yellow Paladin's Bayard, the shoulder cannon can take out a fleet of enemy ships with just one blast.

THE TEAM

It's not just the Paladins of Voltron who fight for justice in the universe. Along with a secret Galra society, the remaining Alteans, and the rapidly growing Voltron alliance, the universe is being freed from evil. Next you will meet the team that comes together to defend the universe.

KING ALFOR

King Alfor was a gifted leader
and alchemist. Before his death,
Alfor scattered the lions across
the universe to keep Voltron away
from the Galra. After awaking from
a ten-thousand-year cryo-sleep,
Princess Allura used her father's
memories to guide her in the fight
against the Galra. However, the
memories were corrupted. Allura
was forced to erase him and lead
on her own. Alfor's dream lives
on through the Paladins. His
legacy is Voltron.

PRINCESS ALLURA

Princess Allura is the last surviving member of the Altean royal family and the teenage daughter of King Alfor. Allura slept in a cryo-pod for ten thousand years. Presently, Princess Allura leads the charge against the Galra Empire.

Like her father, Allura is a gifted diplomat and a fierce leader.

STRENGTH //////////////////

AGILITY //////////////////////

INTELLIGENCE /////////////////////////

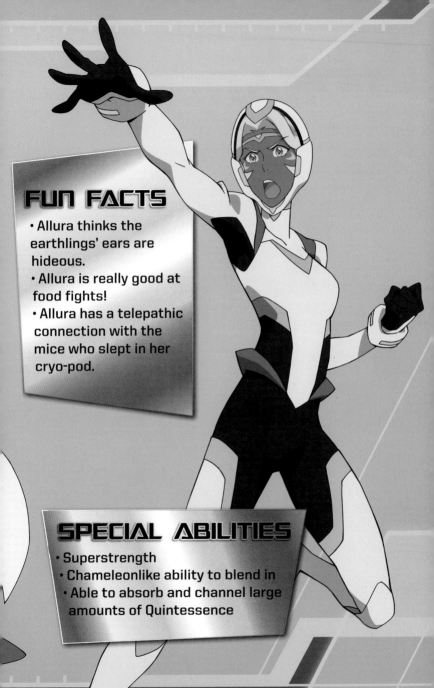

FUN FACTS

- Allura thinks the earthlings' ears are hideous.
- Allura is really good at food fights!
- Allura has a telepathic connection with the mice who slept in her cryo-pod.

SPECIAL ABILITIES

- Superstrength
- Chameleonlike ability to blend in
- Able to absorb and channel large amounts of Quintessence

CORAN

Coran is Princess Allura's trusted advisor. He also cryo-slept for ten thousand years.

STRENGTH //////////////////////
AGILITY //////////////////////
INTELLIGENCE //////////////////////

FUN FACTS

- Full name: Coran Hieronymus Wimbleton Smythe
- Coran's grandfather built the Castle of Lions 10,600 years ago.
- Coran has an encyclopedic knowledge of the known universe.

Do not be intimidated by my energetic expertise and ageless beauty. I am as much a counselor to the Paladins as I am to Allura. As such, I remain both hip and "with it" at all times. In fact, I was considered a bit of an intergalactic fashion pirate in my day. I used to have a bolwaggle cape that I trained to sing my theme song whenever I entered a room!

THE GALRA EMPIRE

DUN-DUN-DUN . . . WHAT? WE CAN'T HAVE SCARY SPACE MUSIC? I FEEL LIKE A SECTION ON THE GALRA NEEDS SOME SCARY SPACE MUSIC.

The Galra Empire is a massive, controlling imperium that rules most of the known universe. It is led by Emperor Zarkon and his quest for ultimate power and vengeance.

/generally

The Galra are a militant, combative people. Galra soldiers rise through the ranks via combat and are honor bound to never turn down a challenge. They seek to avenge their destroyed planet.

A BRIEF HIERARCHY OF THE GALRA EMPIRE

- Emperor Zarkon
- Haggar and the Druids
- Zarkon's commanders
- Galra warriors
- Sentries (robots)
- Conquered civilizations across the universe

That are very easy to hack!

EMPEROR ZARKON

Lord of the known universe

Formerly: friend of King Alfor; original Black Paladin

Age: more than ten thousand years old

Wants: to capture Voltron

Voltron is the only weapon that can stop him.

Zarkon has been the ruthless leader of the Galra Empire for more than ten thousand years. His impressive longevity is due to an overconsumption of Quintessence.

After the destruction of his home planet, Zarkon vowed to avenge it. He now travels across the universe, enslaving weaker civilizations. He forces them to support his empire and give up their resources.

As the original Paladin of the Black Lion, Zarkon maintains a strong psychic bond with it.

STRENGTH ////////////////////////
INTELLECT ////////////////////////
WICKEDNESS ////////////////////////

HAGGAR

- witch allied with the Galra
- former Altean scientist
- leader of the Druids

Haggar is a mysterious witch and leader of the Druids, who are aligned with the Galra Empire. Recently, she revealed herself to be Altean—something that surprised even Princess Allura.

Coran and I thought we were the last Alteans alive!

Haggar has a strange connection to Emperor Zarkon. We aren't quite sure what her role is in the Galra Empire, but it is clear she is a trusted advisor and personal counselor to Zarkon himself. Haggar's powers are great. She harnesses Quintessence to create Robeasts from Zarkon's traitors. She is able to make copies of herself at will and is the reason that Shiro has a robotic arm.

STRENGTH ///////////////////////

INTELLECT ///////////////////////

WICKEDNESS ///////////////////////

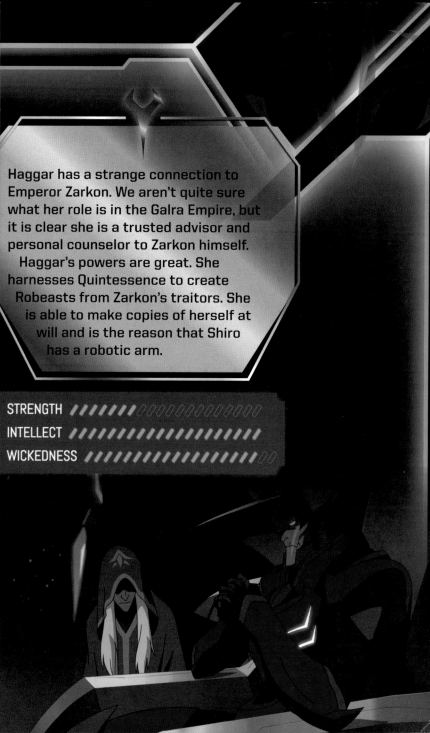

THE DRUIDS

AS YOU CAN SEE, THE DRUIDS REALLY LIKE TO WEAR PURPLE. WHO KNEW PURPLE WAS THE COLOR OF GALACTIC EVIL?

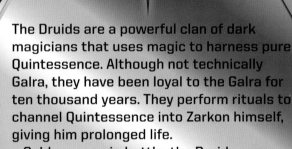

The Druids are a powerful clan of dark magicians that uses magic to harness pure Quintessence. Although not technically Galra, they have been loyal to the Galra for ten thousand years. They perform rituals to channel Quintessence into Zarkon himself, giving him prolonged life.

Seldom seen in battle, the Druids are fierce fighters nonetheless.

The Druids are responsible for the Komar Experiment. This machine took the Druids many deca-phoebs to create. It extracts pure Quintessence from planets and leaves them destroyed and weak.

COMMANDER SENDAK

- commander in Emperor Zarkon's army
- trained by Emperor Zarkon

Like Shiro, Sendak wields a mighty robotic arm created by Haggar and the Druids. The arm is extremely powerful in combat. However, unlike Shiro, Sendak's arm is an "upgraded" version—it can also extend.

Beyond his physical abilities, Sendak is a skilled warrior. Not too long ago, the Paladins captured Sendak. After a failed attempt to search his memories for information, Shiro ejected Sendak into space.

STRENGTH ///////////////////////

INTELLECT ////////////////////

WICKEDNESS ////////////////////

COMMANDER PROROK

former high-ranking commander in Emperor Zarkon's army
• former Galra Robeast

Commander Prorok was a vile enemy whose pride and militancy was so dangerous, he once tried to capture Voltron alone—against Zarkon's wishes.

Thankfully, Prorok is no longer a threat. Although Prorok was loyal to the Galra, Zarkon feared he was trying to sabotage them. With the witch Haggar's magic, Prorok was turned into a fierce Robeast.

Later, Prorok the Robeast was killed by Ulaz, a Marmora operative.

See "Ulaz" file on page 55.

ROBEASTS

The Robeasts are created by Haggar to serve the Galra Empire. They are not quite robot and not quite beast. They are made from Zarkon's traitors, transformed by Quintessence and weaponized with Galra tech, like the former Commander Prorok.

No two Robeasts are the same. Some are larger than Voltron. Some shoot lasers while others devour everything in their path. They are launched from Zarkon's home base in coffin-like ships. When they arrive at their coordinates, they attack until their mission is complete. The mission is always to annihilate.

I wonder if this what Haggar had mind for me, bef I escaped.

PRINCE LOTOR

No way! I have to know what shampoo he is using. If anyone is going to win the award for best hair in the univesre, it's me. Oh, it is ON, Lotor. It. Is. On.

Like his shampoo. I mean, come on.

We actually don't know anything about Prince Lotor yet. If you find any information, young Paladin, please record it here! This is very important to our mission!

THE BLADE OF MARMORA

A mystical, secret legion of Galra resistance fighters. Their motto is "knowledge or death."

ABOUT THE BLADE OF MARMORA

As we have learned, the Galra are not all born with a thirst for power. Some followed Zarkon down his dark path toward dominance; others formed an underground resistance known as the "Blade of Marmora."

Now deca-phoebs old, the Blade of Marmora plants spies in Zarkon's army. They also operate secret outposts and bases hidden throughout the universe.

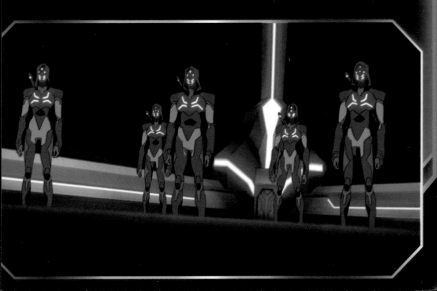

Each member carries a ceremonial blade. The blades are made of Luxite, which is mined from a planet that was destroyed a long time ago. The society operates in secret and knows the secrecy of their organization is of the utmost importance.

Members of the Blade of Marmora are often simply referred to as "blades." They wear ceremonial masks to hide their identities, even among themselves.

THE TRIALS OF MARMORA

To join the Blade of Marmora, prospective blades must pass a rigorous trial. The trial ends in one of two things—knowledge or death. The trial is a deadly battle during which potential members must activate their blades. Two qualifications must be met for the weapon to awaken: Its wielder must show true self-discipline, and the wielder must be of Galra descent.

Our own Keith underwent the trials not too long ago. Only when Keith chose to give up his blade did it awaken.

Keith is now a member of the Blade of Marmora.

EAH, BUT BODY COULD DO THAT, RIGHT?

No.

KOLIVAN

Leader of the Blade of Marmora

A stern and dedicated leader, Kolivan stands by the tenants of the Blade of Marmora. To earn his trust, you must follow his rules entirely. He has lost many of his operatives in the fight against Zarkon, and he honors them by protecting those who remain.

Initially skeptical of the Paladins, Kolivan was won over when Keith passed the Trials of Marmora. He is an essential ally of the Voltron alliance.

ULAZ

- former Galra soldier
- undercover operative for the Blade of Marmora

We owe everything to Ulaz.

Ulaz was a soldier in Zarkon's army. However, he was also a secret member of the Blade of Marmora.

While undercover, Ulaz encountered an interesting prisoner from planet Earth: Shiro. Earth was where the Blue Lion was hidden, and the Galra had just learned of its location.

Ulaz did some investigating and learned that Shiro was a gifted pilot and excellent in combat. In a brave move, Ulaz stole the Blue Lion's location coordinates and programmed them into Shiro's robotic arm. Ulaz freed Shiro and urged him to return to Earth to recover the Blue Lion. Then he disappeared to protect his own life.

The Paladins later encountered Ulaz at the Marmora communications base, Thaldycon. It was there that Ulaz saved everyone from one of Zarkon's Robeasts, sacrificing himself in the fight.

THACE

- former Galra commander
- undercover operative for the Blade of Marmora

Working from within Emperor Zarkon's army, Thace often put himself in harm's way to rebel against the Galra Empire.

During the battle with Zarkon for the Black Lion, Thace brought down the energy shield that had all the Paladins and their ships trapped. Emperor Zarkon wrongly identified Commander Prorok as the traitor and transformed him into a Robeast.

Ha-ha! Take that, Zarkon!

Thace was then promoted to Prorok's position. However, during the Paladins' second major battle with Zarkon, Thace caused a power surge in his Galra ship, saving Keith but sacrificing his own life.

ANTOK

Antok was a fearless blade and warrior. He was known to have Kolivan's back—often acting as an aide and counselor to him. Unfortunately, Antok was tragically killed by a Druid when the Paladins fought Haggar. We carry Antok in our hearts as we continue the fight.

EXPLORE THE UNIVERSE

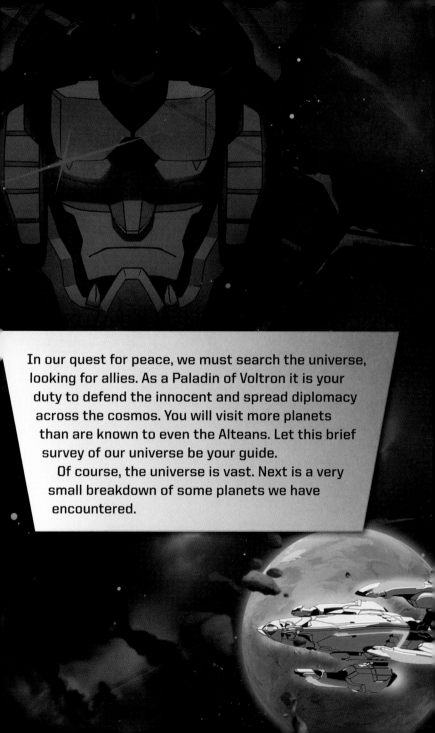

In our quest for peace, we must search the universe, looking for allies. As a Paladin of Voltron it is your duty to defend the innocent and spread diplomacy across the cosmos. You will visit more planets than are known to even the Alteans. Let this brief survey of our universe be your guide.

Of course, the universe is vast. Next is a very small breakdown of some planets we have encountered.

THE ALTEAN CASTLE OF LIONS

The Altean Castle of Lions, also known as the Castleship, is an advanced Altean battleship that can't be explained by science alone.

The Altean Castle of Lions is both a castle and ship, built 10,600 years ago by Coran's grandfather. The ship can only be helmed by a member of the Altean royal family. It is the royal Altean life force that allows the ship to form wormholes. The main engines are powered by Balmera crystals.

AREAS OF THE SHIP INCLUDE

- bridge
- cryo-pods (cryo-pods kept Princess Allura and Coran alive for ten thousand years after Zarkon destroyed Altea)
- training deck with sparring bots and invisible maze
- kitchen and galley
- sleeping quarters
- lounge
- pool
- infirmary
- library
- ballroom
- holodeck interface
- lion hangars
- shuttle bay with pods
- brig

CAPABILITIES

- particle barrier with weapons system
- artificial gravity and life support systems
- cryo-stasis

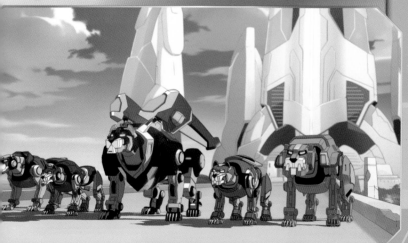

ARUS

The Arusians are a civilization of brave & HUGGABLE! warriors. They ask forgiveness through dance, and show shame through sacrifice. They are unfamiliar with technology, but are steeped in tradition.

Since the Castle of Lions landed on their home planet of Arus ten thousand years ago, the Arusians have passed the story of the Lion Goddess Altura down from one generation to the next. They believed the Black Lion to be a deity, and when the Paladins formed Voltron, it seemed to them that their goddess had been angered.

It was through this early interaction that Princess Allura taught the Paladins about their duty to spread diplomacy throughout the galaxy. Upon departing the planet, Allura gave the Arusian king a communicator to summon the Paladins whenever he needed assistance.

Arus was the first planet in the Voltron alliance.

Arusians celebrate by saying "hoo-rah!" It's a rousing cheer.

THE BALMERA

The Balmera are planet-size creatures. These petrified animals produce crystals used to power ships.

Balmerans are a peaceful, humanoid species who dwell in harmony on the Balmera. Balmeran civilizations communicate psychically with and through the Balmera by placing their hands against it.

SOME OF THEM ARE ALSO REALLY PRETTY.

To the Alteans, this species is sacred. The creatures willingly give crystals to our people. In return we perform a rejuvenation ceremony in which we give Quintessence to the Balmera.

The Galra simply take crystals from the Balmera until it perishes. Before the Paladins helped out, the Galra ruled the Balmerans and forced them to mine away their beloved homes.

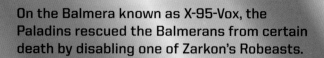

On the Balmera known as X-95-Vox, the Paladins rescued the Balmerans from certain death by disabling one of Zarkon's Robeasts.

Those Balmerans include:

Shay
A kind and hopeful Balmeran who has quite a thing for Hunk.

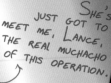

She's just got to meet me, Lance, the real muchacho of this operation.

Rax
Shay's brother, who did not like Hunk or the Voltron Paladins at first.

Shay and Rax's grandmother and parents also live on X-95-Vox.

While defeating the Robeast, Princess Allura performed the sacred ceremony rescuing the Balmera itself from the brink of death. As such, the Balmerans are now allies in the fight against the Galra Empire.

THE BAKU

Lance and Hunk discovered the Village of Baku while torn away from the other Paladins after a fight with Emperor Zarkon.

The Baku is hidden beneath the ice of a watery planet and ruled by Queen Luxia, a beautiful mermaid. Queen Luxia promises all who come to her land will be safe and warm.

However, Lance and Hunk soon discovered that Queen Luxia's people were the victims of mind control. If anyone betrayed her, they were sent to "walk" in the Baku garden, which meant they would be absorbed by the garden and never be seen again.

Thanks to the action of the renegades and Paladins, it was discovered that the garden itself was controlling the minds of the merpeople, including Queen Luxia. The garden was in fact a gigantic alien sea serpent—not a benevolent land.

The Blue Lion activated its Sonic Cannon to free Queen Luxia's people from its spell. They have lived in peace with the Voltron alliance ever since.

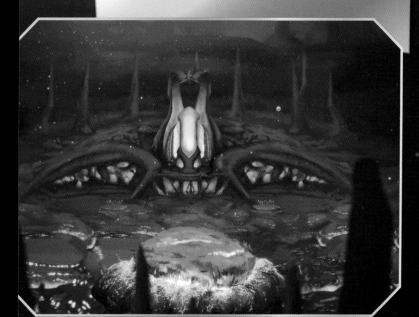

THE MERPEOPLE OF THE VILLAGE OF BAKU

QUEEN LUXIA

A benevolent leader and beautiful mermaid, Queen Luxia was accidentally an unwitting participant in the Baku's plan. She unknowingly forced her people to be brainwashed by the Baku. Once freed, she vowed to protect others and joined the Voltron alliance.

So beautiful she could be → Mrs. Blue Lion.

PLAXUM, BLUMFUMP, AND SWIRN

These were the valiant rebels in the Baku village, who did not fall prey to the Baku's brainwashing. It was thanks to Plaxum, Blumfump, and Swirn that Hunk and Lance were able to fight the sea serpent.

TAUJEER

The planet of Taujeer has a solid shell that periodically sheds, revealing its churning acid center. However, the Taujeerians, a peaceful and technologically advanced people, had prepared for the eventual and natural shedding of their planet's outer layer. They had created a settlement on higher ground and built an Ark. As such, many Taujeerians had never seen the light of day before!

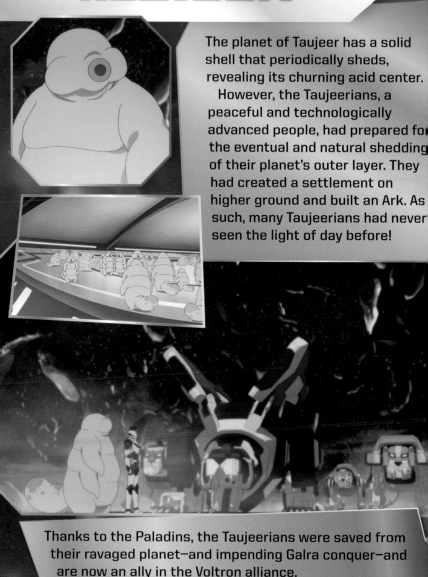

Thanks to the Paladins, the Taujeerians were saved from their ravaged planet—and impending Galra conquer—and are now an ally in the Voltron alliance.

SPACE MALL

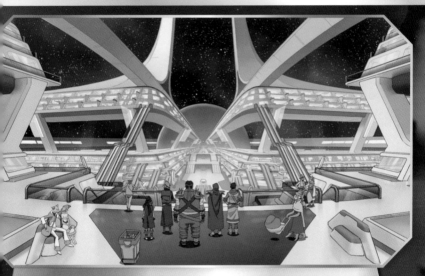

Turn the page to read about the different stops in the Space Mall.

The Space Mall evolved out of swap moons run by the Unilu. The Unilu are traders and pirates who roam the galaxies and deal in black-market goods like Umvy spice, by-tor water, and little bottles of infinity vapor. Be warned: the Unilu are excellent bargainers, but who can pass up a deal?

I once gave away three-quarters of my shipment of lango in exchange for a used pogo oscillator. King Alfor was not happy about that.

VREPIT SAL'S SUSTENANCE STAND

REMEMBER THAT NOTHING IS FREE AT VREPIT SAL'S.

The name of this diner sounds a lot like "vrepit sa," the Galra phrase. It is run by a Galra small business owner, Vrepit Sal.

Sal serves unappetizing "sustenance units" prepared by robot chefs. Hunk was so excited to eat something that wasn't food goo, he accidentally got suckered in to being one of Sal's dishwashers when he couldn't pay. Hunk wasn't content to wash dishes, though. Sal promoted him to a kitchen chef.

As chef, Hunk used his culinary genius to make Vrepit Sal's the best eatery in the galaxy. However, Hunk soon returned to defending the universe as a Paladin of Voltron. Rumor has it

IT'S EARTH

If you find yourself missing Earth, young Paladin, It's Earth in the Space Mall is where to go. This store boasts an impressive collection of worthless Earth memorabilia. One could purchase a video game called Killbot Phantasm One or Gameplayer Five (with the original power glove that gives you infinite lives) for twelve thousand GAC. Of course, why would anyone pay twelve thousand GAC for that? Ha-ha-ha.

Yeah, why would anyone do that. . . .

It is not advisable to make a purchase from this store. The tech is completely incompatible with Altean energy, even though a live Kaltenecker comes free with every purchase. The Paladins call these beastly creatures "cows."

I call them "milk shake makers."

UNILU
SWAP SHOP

This swap shop is what some earthlings might call "old school." Here, you can trade or bargain for anything you might need.

But don't be fooled—when the Unilu offers you a whole case for your firstborn child, it might sound like a good deal, but a savvy swapper can always lower the price.

Like scaultrite lenses.

VARKON

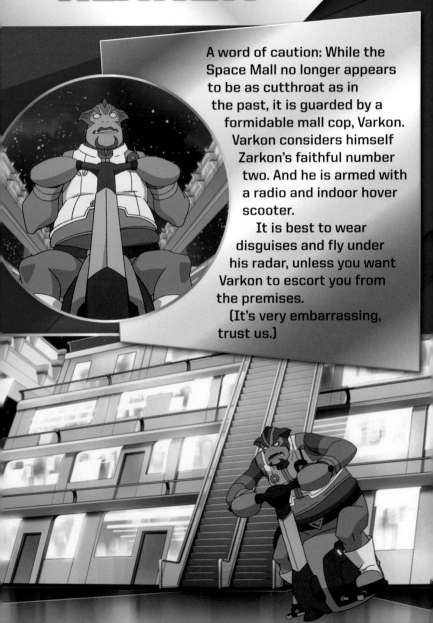

A word of caution: While the Space Mall no longer appears to be as cutthroat as in the past, it is guarded by a formidable mall cop, Varkon. Varkon considers himself Zarkon's faithful number two. And he is armed with a radio and indoor hover scooter.

It is best to wear disguises and fly under his radar, unless you want Varkon to escort you from the premises.

(It's very embarrassing, trust us.)

ALTEA

Although Planet Altea is no more, its legacy lives on. Altea was once a lush and beautiful planet. It was governed by a royal family, including King Alfor; his only daughter, Allura; and Allura's mother.

Weather-wise, Altea did not have wet rain, but had rocks that rained down. It was also full of beautiful flowers, much to the young princess Allura's delight.

The Altean people have distinct marks on their faces, which is how Allura learned that Haggar is Altean. There were also mice on Planet Altea, such as the mice that slept in the same cryo-pod as the princess: ChuChule, Chulatt, Plachu, and Platt.

THE GALAXY GARRISON

Way over yonder, on planet Earth, is the Galaxy Garrison. The Galaxy Garrison is a space exploration and training facility. Isolated in a desolate desert, it is quite advanced by human standards and follows the organization methods of a modern human military.

All the current Paladins roamed the Garrison halls at some point in their careers. Prior to becoming Paladins, Lance, Hunk, and Pidge were active students there. Shiro graduated from the Garrison a few years back, along with Pidge's brother, Matt Holt. Keith was the Garrison's star fighter pilot, but he was let go for disciplinary issues.

And then Lance came in! Booyah.

"Galaxy Garrison exists to turn young cadets like you into the next generation of elite astro-explorers."
–*Commander Iverson, instructor*

MAIN BASE FACILITIES

- satellite communication
- simulator rooms
- classrooms
- dormitories
- instructors' lounge

GALAXY GARRISON CONFIDENTIAL

The Kerberos Mission File

Kerberos: moon orbiting Pluto
Mission Objective: extract ice samples from the surface of the moon and analyze them for signs of alien life
Personnel: Mission Commander and Senior Science Officer Samuel "Sam" Holt; Junior Science Officer Matthew "Matt" Holt; Pilot Takashi "Shiro" Shirogane
Status: incomplete

Mission Notes

When the Kerberos team reached the moon, it signified the farthest humans had ever traveled from Earth. Launch, journey, and landing went smoothly. The space explorers had already started extracting samples when communication with Galaxy Garrison ceased. A rescue mission recovered the ship, rover, and sample collection gear intact, but the personnel were not found. Official cause of mission failure has been deemed human error.

Update

It is now believed that the astronauts were captured by the Galra Empire. If true, this proves human interaction with alien life. Shiro returned to Earth a year later with a cybernetic prosthetic, but disappeared soon after. Matt and Sam Holt remain missing, presumed dead.

LEARN TO SPEAK ALTEAN

Earthlings have some, well, rather . . . *odd* phrases. Next you will learn the *real* language of the the Voltron Paladins— Altean, of course!

MEASUREMENTS OF TIME

TRANSLATED TO APPROXIMATE EARTH UNITS

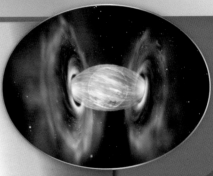

- **Deca-Phoeb:** year
- **Phoeb:** month
- **Movement:** week
- **Quintant:** day
- **Varga:** hour
- **Dobosh:** minute
- **Tick:** a tad longer than a second

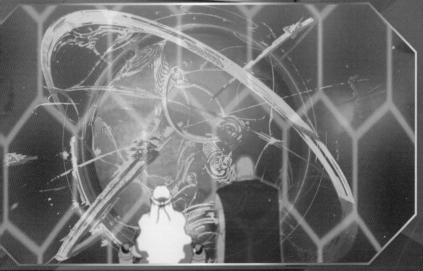

ANIMALS

(as described by Pidge) *REALLY SCARY*

- ***Klamüirl:*** bearlike creature with antennae and a third eye that appears when provoked

- ***Xznly Squiwl:*** an enormous crab-like creature with ferocious teeth and giant claws

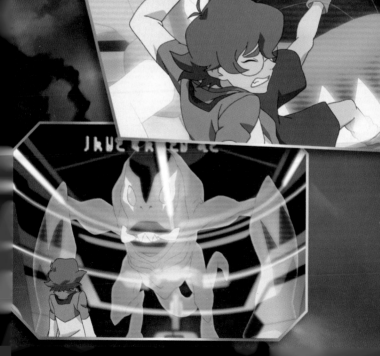

GENERAL SPACE TERMS

- **Sloven-day-ho:** gone
- **Quiznak:** a word uttered during moments of extreme stress, anger, or anxiety. Please refrain from using such language if possible.

IMPORTANT GALRA PHRASE

- **Vrepit sa!:** military salute showing allegiance to Zarkon

IMPORTANT INFORMATION FOR YOUR PALADIN JOURNEY

Of course, being a Paladin of Voltron isn't just exploring new worlds and battling Robeasts. It's also about staying knowledgeable on many things in the universe. Next, you will find some additional information for your Paladin journey. As you venture off to faraway worlds, you are welcome to add your *own* notes in the margins!

QUINTESSENCE

Quintessence powers the lions of Voltron and is the secret to Zarkon's ten-thousand-year life. The Druids harvest Quintessence from planets and channel it into their leader. Quintessence creates an unquenchable thirst for more power. Zarkon never ceases his search for it, harvesting it wherever he can.

THE TELUDAV

The Teludav is an essential piece of the Altean Castle of Lion's mechanics. Using the energy of Princess Allura, or another member of the Altean royal family, it creates wormholes for the ship to travel through.

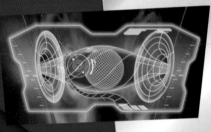

Note: The Teludav cannot function, however, without Scaultrite Lenses perfectly arranged to reflect Allura's energy and form wormholes. This has proved troublesome in the past.

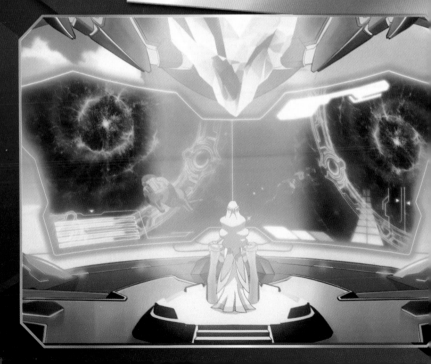

FRAUNHOFER LINES

A Fraunhofer line shows the emission spectrum of an element. These spectral lines were the key to the recovery of the Blue Lion (and, ultimately, Voltron). We have Hunk to thank for this!

After reviewing Pidge's notes on alien activity, Hunk recognized a repeating series of numbers as the emission signature of a mysterious element. He charted the spectral lines to try to figure out what it was.

MY PRIVATE notes, I should add.

Hunk showed the chart to Keith, who made the connection between the shape of the wavelength and the mountains around the cave where the Blue Lion was hidden. Once the team was inside the cave, the Blue Lion revealed itself to Lance!

Fraunhofer lines are VERY important, young Paladin.

WEBLUM

The Weblum is an enormous space-dwelling worm. It may sound disgusting, but this magnificent creature plays a vit role in universe.

Weblums are one of our last remaining sources of Scaultrite The Weblums secrete Scaultrite as part of their natural defense: and that Scaultrite is used to make the lenses of the Teludav.

TO COLLECT SCAULTRITE FROM A WEBLUM

- use the Altean Weblum finder to locate a Weblum
- find the Weblum's blind spot at the back of the neck and enter through the gills
- get to the third stomach and find the Scaultrite gland
- activate the Weblum's defense mechanisms and collect the excess Scaultrite
- the simplest exit from the Weblum is the least pleasant

LET'S JUST SAY YOU'LL GET TAKEN OUT WITH THE TRASH.

Remember, stay away from its face! Otherwise, it'll shoot a venomous las out of its mouth, directly at you. Als avoid its internal natural defenses and deadly acid. This creature is basically a death monster.
Happy collecting!

Congratulations, Paladin!

Now that you've finished this handbook, it is time to learn which lion *you* will pilot as a Paladin of Voltron. Please answer all questions honestly, and go with your gut! Remember—the lion chooses you.

QUIZ: WHICH LION WILL YOU PILOT AS A PALADIN OF VOLTRON?

1. Which food do you miss most from Planet Earth?

A.   Hearty, home-cooked meals
B.   Fast food, ready at the counter
C.   Peanut butter and jelly sandwiches
D.   Cheese! Pizza, grilled cheese, fondue. Mmm.
E.   All of it!

2. You're going on an unknown mission and can only pack one thing. What do you bring?

A.   Map
B.   Knife
C.   Rope
D.   Matches
E.   Shield

3. You're going to cryo-sleep for ten thousand years. Which animal do you hope shares your cryo-pod?

A.   Cat
B.   Hippopotamus
C.   Owl
D.   Shark
E.   Dog

4. What is your biggest strength in battle?

A.   Leadership
B.   Instinct
C.   Creativity
D.   Boldness
E.   Compassion

5. If you could have any superpower, what would it be?

A. Invisibility
B. Superspeed
C. Mind control
D. Flight
E. X-ray vision

6. What would you hope to buy at the Space Mall?

A. A few things for my backpack, maybe a new pair of socks.
B. Nothing. I'd like to browse the mall directory, though.
C. Something fun that reminds me of home, like a video game! Or a chess set.
D. Fuzzy space slippers, of course.
E. Buy? I don't have any GAC to spend.

7. You have some free time aboard the Castleship. What are you doing?

A. Working. There's always more to plan when it comes to Zarkon.
B. Heading to the pool! Time to relax.
C. Studying, maybe fiddling around with a few things.
D. Snoozing. I'll stay right in bed, thanks.
E. Collecting ingredients for tonight's dinner, which is going to be amazeballs, by the way.

8. A magical wormhole will take you to any planet, where you will live the rest of your life in peace. Where do you choose?

A. Nowhere. There's always more work to be done. I have to make sure we defend the universe.
B. Somewhere wild and fiery—I wouldn't mind a volcano.
C. A grassy, peaceful planet sounds nice.
D. Earth. They've got the best Italian food in the galaxy.
E. I don't mind which planet I'm on, so long as I'm with those I love.

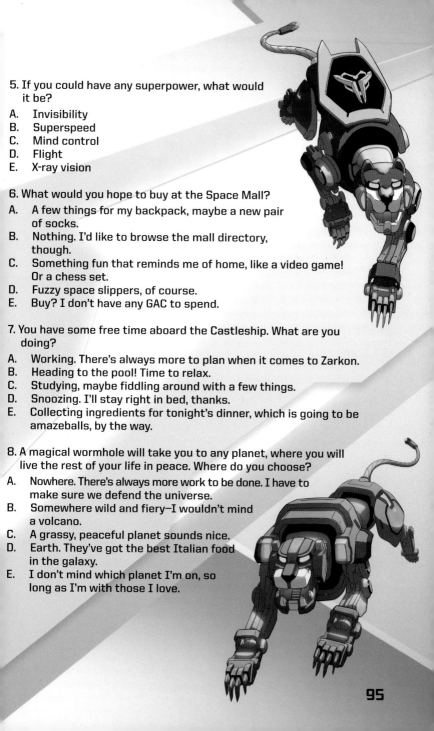

9. You have an important test coming up. How do you prepare?

A. Chill out; listen to some music. I've already prepared and need a clear head.

B. I'll tackle the test when the time comes—I'm not too good at studying.

C. A test? This week's or next week's? This week I've already taken two practice tests that predict a score of 97 or higher.

D. I might open the textbook for a second or two.

E. I'll study, but I get so nervous during test time, I might throw up.

10. What do you value most?

A. Teamwork
B. Honor
C. Wisdom
D. Confidence
E. Quick thinking

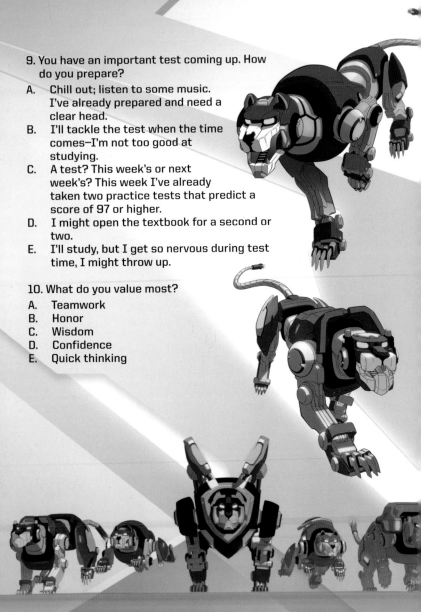

If you answered:
mostly As, you should pilot the Black Lion; mostly Bs, you should pilot the Red Lion; mostly Cs, you should pilot the Green Lion; mostly Ds, you should pilot the Blue Lion; mostly Es, you should pilot the Yellow Lion.